PRAISE FOR JUNE AKERS SEESE

What Waiting Really Means

"There is a brittle sadness to the life of this woman, who admits she was never ready for middle age. But there is also humor and an enigmatic kind of insight. . . . *What Waiting Really Means* is a promising debut novel."

—*Atlanta Journal and Constitution*

Is This What Other Women Feel Too?

"Touching—at times jarring. . . . From bra-stuffing to Janis Joplin, e. e. cummings to Lenny Bruce, Neutrogena soap to the race riots in Detroit, well-chosen details give texture to the characters' lives. Kate's depression is painful but her attitude never entirely humorless, and the counterpoint between her sometimes resigned, generally cynical (but always intelligent) voice and the snappy letters from Parker keeps the pace brisk."

—*Publishers Weekly*

James Mason and the Walk-in Closet

"The stories and two novellas in this unsentimental collection emphasize mood and tone over action and expertly convey a mature, weary, middle-aged female sensibility."

—*Cleveland Plain Dealer*

OTHER BOOKS BY JUNE AKERS SEESE

Is This What Other Women Feel Too?
James Mason and the Walk-in Closet

JUNE
AKERS
SEESE

what waiting really means

Dalkey Archive Press
NORMAL · LONDON

Cover: *Romona's Bust* by René Guerin. Photographed by J. D. Scott.

Library of Congress Cataloging-in-Publication Data:

Seese, June Akers, 1935–
    What waiting really means / June Akers Seese.— 1st ed.
    I. Title.
PS3569.E356W4   1990   813'.54—dc20   89-27251
ISBN 1-56478-394-4

Partially funded by grants from the National Endowment for the Arts,
a federal agency, and the Illinois Arts Council, a state agency.

Dalkey Archive Press is a nonprofit organization located at Milner Library
(Illinois State University) and distributed in the UK by
Turnaround Publisher Services Ltd. (London).

www.centerforbookculture.org

Printed on permanent/durable acid-free paper and bound in the
United States of America.

Contents

What Waiting Really Means

I

Big Plans in Detroit

I n the neighborhood where I grew up, women didn't work. A few tried, but their plans backfired. My mother was one of them. She got a job in an airplane factory running a drill press, but she was allergic to the metal dips. I'll let you imagine what her hands looked like.

At the end of our block, near the bus stop, two prissy girls lived in a one-bedroom house with their mother. She kept her job a secret until she got to know you. They were Jehovah's Witnesses and had their eyes on the end of the world. But for now, their mother wore white cotton gloves, weekdays, summer and winter. I'll let you imagine what her hands looked like, too. She was a maid. She didn't have a husband to stop her; rubber gloves had vanished in the war effort. It was 1944.

I have to think hard to remember those crooked streets and how muddy they were in the spring. I didn't know what "white trash" meant then, but there was no shortage on our block. The main difference between people who got ahead and those who didn't was a matter of nerves. White trash could relax. They didn't have flower beds to weed or houses to paint. They rented and moved on. Holding down two jobs seemed crazy to them. When they were sick, they stayed home. They also had an affinity for forbidden animals—chickens and rabbits. Their kids petted them and took them indoors where they might show up on the Sunday dinner table with milk gravy.

Years later, I realized what *dumb* meant. Dumb people live in the here and now. They have more children than they should, and they don't save money.

Sometimes I wish I could go back because I don't enjoy a thing I own, and my head shakes if someone asks me two questions at the same time. I'd like to be spared the misery a lifetime of planning and waiting has brought me. Maybe I couldn't take the bad grammar and Saturday night fights, but I'd try. I'd like to be sixteen again and "give in." I got screwed anyway, but it wasn't in the backseat of a Chevy. And I'm not talking about sex.

I worked too hard in college and ended up at General Motors, in spite of myself. Grand Boulevard is not so grand when you finally get there. My office is on the eighth floor, and I have a secretary who can afford suits from I. Magnin. The feminists would welcome me with open arms if I took a walk in their direction, but I see through yuppies and old houses with potential; and the only time I run is if someone is chasing me. Protest marches leave me cold, too. Jimmy Hoffa ended up in a Dempsey Dumpster, and I saw Walter Reuther's bloody shoulder firsthand!

Consider this: Once, on my aunt's screened porch, a Mexican numbers runner who worked for my uncle at the steel mill hugged me and rubbed my nipples into his shirt. I was twelve years old and green as grass. My heart pounds thinking of it.

And this: Four years later I was kissed into a frenzy by the captain of the football team. My blouse hung on the steering wheel. "No," I said, and meant it. The future beckoned.

This too: Men who wear Brooks Brothers suits and pretend to read books are a step backward, and not far enough back, at that. I'd be better off reading a Victorian novel where set patterns and places bring a little consolation and the story line goes somewhere. Upward mobility sucks!

II

Your Mother and Mine

The other day I got into a fight with my best friend over a word. We were playing "Can You Top This" with our pasts. In the end, I told too much. These deathbed scenes are new to me. My family leaves this world fast. My uncle died in a parking lot, and my mother slept too late one morning.

I visit Margaret every day after lunch. The nurses don't like it. "Nap time," they say. Margaret claims she's let her children take enough naps for the whole family. She has eight and a husband who has held up. They're Catholic. She could have kept right on going. In childbirth, the pelvis is everything.

Words are important, too. None of us says CANCER out loud, but in my dream it appears on billboards and is dragged through the March sky in puffy letters. Margaret doesn't talk about her dreams—which brings me to the word we fought over, *embarrass-ment*. For years we traded stories about our mothers —one eccentric and one almost crazy—but we stopped in time. Monday was different. We inter-rupted each other and turned red. The nurses made me leave early.

When I came back today, there was an empty room and a toothless woman with a can of Lysol. In a few minutes I realized what had happened. There was not a nurse in sight. I was glad to miss the priest, an effeminate man with lace cuffs and a cliché for every day of the week. The woman handed me a letter. I didn't read it until I was home in the bathtub. My glasses steamed up, and the envelope fell in the water.

Dear Mary,

My mother's search for pleasure was more than embarrassing. Your mother gave up on pleasure. She embraced morality, work, and the afterlife. She had views on everything, and she was not afraid to tell them. My mother thought the afterlife a hoax and priests out to get your money, but she kept her opinions to herself. She sought out relief, instead, as regularly as if she punched a clock somewhere on the Greyhound Bus Line.

Your mother gave up on femininity. She wore old lady's oxfords when she was thirty and never a trace of cologne. My mother's cupboards were stuffed with earrings and Jungle Gardenia. She flirted with bus drivers and garage mechanics. In some part of town, my father must have been a laughingstock. There is a difference, Mary, between embarrassment and shame. And by the way, where is pleasure to be found?

Love,
Margaret

That's all. The letter explains the fortress she built around herself with those children, but it doesn't satisfy me.

I walked all the way back to the General Motors Building and sat at my desk. I took out a new address book from the closet and began with the A's. My

Rolodex gets lifted from time to time. I was typing "Thompson, James" when I realized it was seven o'clock. I left everything spread across my desk and checked out. On the elevator, going down, my eyes began to water. My allergies are worse in the spring.

There's a bar and a bus stop three doors down. The wind lifted my skirt. I should have worn a coat. I walked in and picked a stool near the back. "Jameson's and a Stroh's." The bartender knows Margaret and John, and he knew my father.

"Mary, St. Patrick's Day is just around the corner." You could take a remark like that to mean anything.

"Bring me another whiskey," I said, and when he did, I grabbed his hands tight enough to draw blood. "She ain't comin' back," I whispered—lapsing into the language of my childhood.

III

Courtship

Three days later, they buried Margaret. I took a cab to the Shrine of the Little Flower and made my way through the gladiolas and the handkerchiefs. Thank God they had another priest. He didn't take long, and I don't remember what he said. On the way to the cemetery, I pulled out a silver flask I had engraved for Margaret, just her first name, on the front. I had a speech prepared about how we'd fool the nurses and drink brandy together right up to the end. Well, now it's mine.

The whole world turned out for the wake. John even invited the builder. He had enough sense to dress up, and he didn't stay long. Neither did I, and when he offered to cancel my cab, I let him. "Whose idea was the diamond lights?" I started up. "How many styles are you using in those windows? Margaret knew the difference between a house and an abortion, and I'd like to see them out of there!" He drove straight through a red light. He didn't say a word but circled the block and left off a bundle of base shoe with his foreman. Margaret and John lived in the first house in a subdivision without trees.

We had dinner at the Ponchartrain Wine Cellars, his idea, and he paid for it. I had trouble talking because he'd never read a book worth mentioning in his life, and there's only so far you can travel on wisecracks. On the way home, he said, "The windows can be fixed." I brightened up.

We were married two months later. Fifty seats. Fifty people. I threw away the dress I got married in. It was thin cotton with an eyelet bodice. My mother made it, and I thought it was the whitest material on the bolt at J. L. Hudson's. I have never been partial to silk.

We skipped the honeymoon. It was all right with me. Spent five days at the Book Cadillac instead, and we went to work every day. It was fun—room service at night and orange juice and a rose in the morning.

I bought new clothes in New York that fall, and we saw the inside of some hotel rooms there, too. He wasn't all slide rules and sawdust, and he could hold his own with the goons from the union. As for the flask and Margaret, he got the point.

IV

Meeting Margaret

I met Margaret at a wedding in Hamtramck. We were stuffing ourselves with piroghi, and her first son was asleep on the floor in the bedroom between a diaper bag that played Brahms's "Lullaby" and a pile of fur coats. We started talking and kept right on through nursing the baby and a conversation on the shortage of sanitation engineers. That one came for free from two drunks in the doorway. When they saw Margaret in the rocker, they left.

"So much for Detroit men. Let's get back to the dancing," I laughed. The bride was counting the cash, and the groom was loaded. They both had a long way to go, and he was out of step. By the end of the evening, Margaret and I were friends. After that, we ate fish and chips out every Friday—give or take a few recessions. John kept the kids in line, and we split the check. In the end, I guess all that greasy newsprint means something.

Margaret with a mantilla over her head, off to Mass. Margaret with her son in her lap in that torn-up kitchen. At night she zipped them all into Doctor Dentons and read the most chilling ghost stories I've ever heard. For Margaret, every day was Halloween. You have to feel safe to enjoy being scared like that.

V

A Boom Town

There were ups and downs. Marriage being what it has always been. But it was much better than blind dates with policemen who thought the world stopped at the cigar stand in the General Motors Building. I couldn't abide white-collar men who aspired to a fake colonial on two lots in Dearborn where that fat bastard gets reelected every year on the strength of his garbage pickup and who he keeps out. I even had a lover who pulled out my diaphragm and threw it against the wall. I am not a liberated woman and I didn't like the imagery. Never mind his reasons. Never mind the package deal: the house at the lake and two sets of dishes to wash. Never mind deer hunting and the nigger jokes. If you drink enough blackberry brandy in the Upper Peninsula, you can convince yourself automobiles and doe season really matter.

My husband is what he is, and he doesn't have to kick somebody's ass to prove it. He spent some time on a bicycle before he left home, and his legs do a lot for me.

Recessions played hell with the building business, but things went along all right until we got greedy and moved to Atlanta. You know the story: cheap labor, sunshine, a boom town and all that goes with it. My husband is out early and late scrambling for contracts. Subdivisions sprout up all over. Skyscrapers are making Marietta something more than a meeting place for the John Birch Society and the Klan. High rises have a beauty of their own.

Specialty work is hard to come by, and his master cabinetmaker comes from Glasgow. I won't tell you what he paid his foreman to relocate. They went to school with Gene Krupa in Hamtramck, and it would take boiling water, in a surprise move, to separate them.

They didn't have to ask me twice to say goodbye to that gray slush and the corroded fenders on Grand

Boulevard. "Won't you miss your family, Mary?" I always liked my bedroom. The locked door. My stack of Charlie Parker records. The white woodwork. The blue wallpaper.

We had a big send-off at Lelli's, and somebody tried to swim in the fountain with the colored lights. Waiters wear tuxedos there, and they are not easy to shock. I drank my share of champagne and leaned on my husband all the way home. We walked. Cabs have their own risks. *The Red Desert* was on TV. My husband called it a clean-cut movie, and he was right. The factory was as stark as the woman's bedroom. It had an eerie feel, and I was glad to be under the quilts listening to the pipes heat up. "Hold me tighter," I giggled. A trumpet player lives in one room across the courtyard, and we keep the windows open. Snow falls in piles on the ledge.

In the middle of the night, I packed my books. "We'll make you bookcases that meet the ceiling," my husband said, touching my face. "Pitch these metal frames."

I did, and I gave away all the exercise equipment

we never use. Then I bought new underwear. That was a mistake. In the South, they pay a lot of attention to cover-ups. And I don't mean cotton panties.

VI

Immortality

My husband made out his will this afternoon. He is forty-seven and healthy as a horse. We were lying in bed, and I thought about his body. There's a chunk missing from his ankle—an old bicycle accident—and a scar across his middle where they took out his gall bladder, but he can climb stairs with the best of them.

We live in a big house on a busy boulevard at the edge of the city. Once it was the Atlanta Conservatory for the Blind. Before that, one family lived in it for forty years. Sometimes, when I am alone at night, I think of those sightless children bumping into the stucco walls in the attic, and I shiver. I'm a practical woman, not given to grieving over the past, even when it is someone else's.

The rooms here are big, the ceilings high, the baseboards made of real mahogany. I have a favorite place in each room. I like to smoke and watch the sun hit the dust in the air. When my husband is away, I take long walks. The city is new to me. I talk to the carpenters and mailmen. It seems everything is being repaired, and there's no shortage of printed words. I have lived long enough to know some things can't be fixed, and this knowledge makes me enjoy the carpenters all the more. I like their bare backs and the smell of wood.

The will scares me. It's like passing an obstacle and finding "nothing" on the other side. I don't want to know what will happen to this house. I don't want to learn more about trusts and taxes. My memories stop with the furniture. Moving vans? Drivers? They are not like the carpenters. Their load is always too heavy. Didn't they drop my love seat?

So I stayed upstairs and left my husband's papers stretched out on the dining-room table. The afternoon passed. I mopped the sleeping porch and fluffed up the comforters. I'm having a go at James Joyce for the third time. I like to reread the Molly Bloom chapter and pretend I have the brains for the rest.

"What have you done with the glasses, Mary?"

I was relieved to hear my name called, and I hurried into a loose dress, holding on to the banister, all the way down. My husband poured some bourbon into teacups, and we went out onto the porch to consider our options. There's a new movie four blocks away from a Korean restaurant with a waterwheel in the window. Sometimes, we have eggs at a diner or listen to a blonde singer who reminds me of Peggy Lee. It's all within walking distance.

I knew my husband wanted to call his foreman. But he didn't. He didn't say anything either. He just picked me up and carried me up the stairs. The wind was blowing the curtains into a frenzy. "The movies can wait," he whispered in my ear. I forgot all about the will and concentrated on the here and now.

VII

Moving On

The difference is that now we stay put. Out-of-town trips are a luxury that have nothing to do with money. This is it. Right here. Janis Joplin drank Southern Comfort and talked straight up: "As we say, out on the terrain, it's all one fucking day, man. Tomorrow never happens."

After the Ellis Theatre, we walk home and sit on the porch. There is a boy, a cupid without the arrows, about three feet tall, plastered into the wall. Water comes out of his mouth when the plumbing works, and drains away around the flowerpots at his feet. We sit in white wicker chairs and consider the red geraniums. The French doors are wide open, and we pay attention to sounds from the street.

We used to ride sleepers to New York City. Detroit was closer, I guess. The blue canopy at Birdland?

Gone, now. The Cherry Lane Theatre? I don't remember the plays, but I remember how I felt—full. There was a bar next to the Cherry Lane, and we closed it up and kept right on going. Bobby Short was forty then, and he still had that book on Cole Porter in his head. Like everything else, it's a matter of focus, and his mind was on the music. There was no need to talk.

We bought gifts for Margaret's kids and that took a whole afternoon. A cast-iron train from F.A.O. Schwartz that made real smoke. A quilt for the smallest ones. A money belt for the oldest. Chocolates for the rest. We ate mangoes in the street and wiped our hands on our clothes. I miss the sloppiness of it.

We weren't in Atlanta a year before something happened to the cabinetmaker. I don't care what, and I don't know why, but he did less and less and finally he disappeared. His wife moved back to Scotland, and we tried to forget about him. You need someone you can depend on.

That's when the fights began. Only they weren't fights. They were orders. I don't mind picking up jockey shorts, but there is a limit. How important is a burned-out light bulb? "Are you going to make a career out of smoking?" He planted his feet on the floor as we were undressing. There's something unnerving about work boots now that everyone is wearing them. What happened to him? The sawdust spilled out of his cuffs, and I sat down and jerked my blouse back on. "You're damn right! And I'm switching to cigars!" I walked all the way to Plaza Drugs and bought three brands. Then I sat at the Majestic Grill and sampled them all. Sounds floated past my head. I needed something stronger than coffee.

When I came back, my husband was asleep on the couch in his undershirt. "Two can play this game." I laid out the V.O. and a water glass and drew a bath. The stream hit the bath oil. I felt as slimy as it looked. I slept in my husband's robe and dreamed about my mother. She was wearing one of her navy blue suits and those hideous flat shoes that were never fashionable. She didn't own a piece of jewelry, but in my dream her wedding ring was wrapped around her ankles and something was pulling her through the snow. I liked the silence of it.

In the morning, I was gone before the alarm went off. Grocery stores open early, and from there I went to the library—with a few stops in-between.

In the library, I saw what I had to look forward to. Retirement. Only I don't have a job. Age ruins your back and plays tricks with your eyes. Some are cavalier about it. Others bitch. Their feverish words spilling onto the paperbacks. Taste is at a premium. Robert Ludlum can't turn them out fast enough, and travel books are biggest for those who can't take trips. The librarians are all depressed, except for one, an aging fashion plate with a mean look on her face. I fit right in.

I have a milk shake for lunch. Fast. At McDonald's. I like the drive-through. It's gone by the time I'm home. It's hard to believe milk is bad for you. I drink it anyway. Heavy. Sweet. I lock the doors and muddle my way through the afternoon. I won't call it a nap. Drifting is a better word. I wish my husband would come home then. Timing is so important and, more and more, clocks bother me. I tossed my Baby Ben in the trash and bought a new radio alarm to drown out the noise in my head. My cigars are never far away.

VIII

Joan Didion and Our Dreams

Have I ever let you down?" he said as the door to the guest room closed. Left behind were his papers in little piles and private arrangements. A nightstand full of tax forms and architect's drawings spread across the coffee table. The lamps turned off and the blinds closed.

"I'm already down. It's a question of leveling off."

How can I tell how bad I feel? Things butt against my skull, and my head still shakes. Outside the fun, and not knowing the games, I sit and look at the trees. The morning glories of my mother's garden have been replaced by hardwoods. This is the South. They don't fool around. They are what they appear to be— all day.

Have you ever seen a mitten frozen in ice? There's order of the best kind.

Behind a window, things seem pretty good. All day, I watch the clock and the pots. They both boil. In the middle of the night the camelback crickets dance on my laundry. Sometimes, when I can't sleep, sitting in a steaming tub, I get a cramp just under my breast. If I lie still, it goes away. I head for the sheets and pull the comforter over my head. My husband turns over. I am damp and naked. Dampness makes things grow. My dreams flourish.

My friend who stayed in Detroit dictates her dreams into a tape recorder the minute she wakes up. She has a job with computers, and she wears a suit every day. The rooms she works in are like caves, and sometimes the air-conditioning makes her sick. Scattered through her head, the thoughts of the morning and afternoon twist and rattle, but the night is safe in that tiny machine.

We have known each other for twenty years. The summer of the riots, we made cream cheese sandwiches for the firemen. We put them on a pewter tray and walked up to the corner, ignoring the smoldering stores along the way. The captain let us know how grateful he was by saying nothing and touching my shoulder. On the way home, I realized the streets were empty, and we were fools. That night the curfew kept us together. We finished off some whiskey and ate the rest of the Wonder Bread. We turned down the sound on the TV and followed the gunfire in the Sears parking lot. It was a basement apartment, and pipes made a pattern on the ceiling. "What do we do with ourselves till this is over?" I said. She turned out the lights and fell asleep before she could answer my question. The riots were beside the point.

My friend calls me from work, and we talk about the weather. She carries a beeper. If one of the computers breaks down, she gets up in the middle of the night to fix it. I guess her dreams wait on those nights. She is patient. Looking for patterns takes time.

We are planning a trip to the beach. We like to watch the waves thunder in when the weather is bad, but she takes Noxema along, just in case. Last summer we read a Joan Didion novel twice. Didion knows all about the frozen mitten—and nightmares, too. "Every day is all there is," she says.

IX

A Love Story

I went crazy. It had been a long time coming. When I look back, I can't place the actual moment. Can anyone? But I do know I couldn't stop talking once I began. I had trouble driving, too. My eyes were drawn to the tape deck. I liked to play the same song over and over. There is a lot of satisfaction in a sure thing.

It was fall, not the golden time in magazines; there was no sun and everything was dying. I read biographies to avoid suspense. In biographies, death is certain and the overall pattern complete.

I was afraid at night. Things spun in my head in circles, and I was aroused the whole time. Once I sat in a tub of hot water and cried. I gave up coffee and drank cup after cup of herbal tea.

Most evenings, I walked from my apartment to

supper. It was a poor neighborhood. I wore heavy lace-up boots, high wool socks, and a corduroy blazer. I was always cold. Sometimes it snowed—thick and steady—and I walked fast. Eight-year-olds passed me on their way to the grocery store, and old men waved from their porches, holding their cigarettes between two fingers.

I looked forward to eating supper. I knew it would be hot. I sat at a table with a priest who had lost a leg to diabetes. He talked about the brothers and his superior at the order. It was dull conversation, but I liked it and I tried to listen.

A tidy life! I washed, dried and folded my clothes after breakfast. I took a nap after lunch. I read to a blind man after supper. I saved the biographies for midnight. Dashiell Hammett was my favorite. Woodie Guthrie, too. Then I lay in bed. I hugged a down pillow my husband had brought me from home and remembered the curve of his back and the feel of his legs.

The snow continued and everybody but the priest began to dress for supper. New people sat at our table. The priest talked about how cold it was in

Minnesota. I kept my mouth shut and chewed my vegetables.

On the weekends I stood in line at the drugstore to get four pills—all I could pay for. A lot of old people were waiting, too. They were angry. Pills cost too much. They, too, could not fill the whole prescription.

I never went to a shopping mall. I avoided the movies. My TV stayed unplugged the whole time. I spent money on books that should have gone for medicine. Although the days were all the same, I never knew what would happen next.

When spring came, the blind man moved away and the priest went back to Minnesota. A biography of Lyndon Johnson lay on the living room rug beside my teacup. I knew all I wanted to know about him. His wife had thick ankles and his heart had failed when he was alone. I had one choice left—Robert Lowell.

So the next night I turned up the heat and pulled the shades. I opened the thick book and examined Lowell's baby pictures, his illustrious family, and a picture of Jean Stafford dressed like a schoolmarm. Lowell was too risky. He had gone mad, too. More than once. And that's what happened to every book I bought or borrowed. Something in it would scare me, and I had to stop reading.

I was left with my dreams. I can't complain. They weren't nightmares. All those stories you hear about going crazy and peculiar dreams and thinking you are somebody else. I always knew who I was—awake or asleep. And, it is true, after so many nights, you do doze off.

Sometime around Valentine's Day, my husband sent me a plane ticket and a red card that played "Sweet Lorraine." My name is Mary, but I know romance when I see it, and I thought about his head. He is bald and handsome. His eyes are dark brown and he always looks tired. I wanted to mash my face into his chest and smell that smell that belongs to nobody else. That's about all I wanted to do, but I felt he'd understand.

I got up the next morning and walked out the door. I left the biographies in a row on the windowsill and my clothes in the closet. The janitor drove me to the airport. He seemed to know something I didn't.

The plane was big. The sun shone. In my seat by the window, I took my medicine with a glass of bourbon. The ice cubes had holes in the center and they hurt my teeth. I counted out two dollars in postage stamps: "My money is in my luggage," I lied.

The stewardess smiled. Her modulated voice and training triumphed: "Will someone be there to meet you?" she whispered.

"Yes," I said, looking at the melting ice. "Someone will be there."

X

What a Wife Is Supposed to Do

I want a wife, not a mistress," my husband told me over the phone. I countered with a word or two about his tomato plants. Sometimes all you have left is one safe topic.

We all have our own ideas about what a mistress is, but I actually met one while I was away—an old-timer, Irish and red-faced. She has her own life too. She writes soap operas and collects lace doilies. A few are framed over her sofa. She is kept by a Jewish businessman. When his wife died, he proposed marriage. "It would ruin everything," she said. He sent her for a face-lift instead.

I was not asking for the world—only an apartment in town—away from the telephone and weeds. I had picked one out. It faced a brick courtyard and bushes that hid the alley. One room and a kitchen—just big enough.

I have never been good at decisions. Finally, I came home and forgot all about separate quarters. Wives have time to stare out windows, and we have windows in every room. I keep hoping my thoughts will come together. So far, all I have to show for my time is a crystal ashtray full of Virginia Slims.

A woman can fill her days with most anything. There are so many choices. I thought I'd be able to make them if I could open the windows and breathe without a repairman explaining my mistakes. Eric Hoffer said, "Maintenance is everything," and he was right. I don't broadcast it, but I like the sound of breaking glass. None of my clothes goes to Goodwill. I stuff them into garbage cans and rush out to the street before the trucks come. I like the sound of the grinder, too. It's spring and nobody notices all those cans in a row. Good-bye. So long. Macramé is a terrible dust catcher.

When you get older, your fingernails break off and curve in. Little ridges you never noticed inch forward on each one. I stare at my hands because I have to.

The wool must be even, the stitches counted. An afghan is a predictable thing. "With the warmer weather, you'll need another hobby," my husband tells me. As long as we're being honest, what I enjoy most is putting the air-conditioner on freeze and spending the afternoon wrapped in an old quilt.

I don't understand what a wife is supposed to do, and the last thing I want is to be a mistress. They wait longer and the timing is more unpredictable. If waiting is all there is, you might as well stay where you are.

XI

Mary at Home

My husband is a reasonable man, but sometimes he lets loose: "All those blue shirts and not a one in my closet when I need it! God damn it, Mary, what do you do all day?" It does no good to point out the pinstripes. More is coming: "The maid is drinking the liquor again. Damn, Mary, don't you know how to deal with N-E-G-R-O-E-S?" By this time he has set out two ties on the dresser and is considering which one looks best. Soon he will be gone. He drives an old Porsche with Recaro seats. You can hear it all the way to Euclid.

It helps to laugh about these early morning outbursts, but my audience is gone. My friends are either divorced or dead. Fresh fruits and vegetables are not what they're cracked up to be, and there was not a smoker in the crowd.

I don't spend much time in the kitchen, but one night last summer I sliced some limes, on an angle, and fanned them out on a crystal plate. We were having new people over who didn't drink. Just as I was pouring ginger ale into a matching pitcher, my husband walked in: "Isn't this just like you, Mary? As long as it looks good, you're happy. It'll lose its fizz! And, those limes. Put some Saran Wrap over them!" I didn't say anything. I walked out the door and drove to a shopping mall. You can be sure I didn't buy a cookbook.

The last few years have been tough. Do I need to say why? Everybody's life is pretty bizarre once you get past the brand names and milestones. We have been married twenty years. In the beginning we were talkers. We talked about the future, the movies. Once we tore *The Godfather* in half so we could read it at the same time and talk about it. Some fast-moving trash, but I sure liked it!

Now we fight. He screams at me, and I step back. I don't know how to play this game.

Sex hasn't changed. It was never bad, but frankly

my favorite place and time is in his arms all night. We don't talk, but neither do we argue.

Nothing prepared me for middle age. I thought it was enough to accept gray hair and wrinkles and a little arthritis in the morning. There are remedies for those things. But distances crop up everywhere. It's hard to feel close to a screamer. The other day, in front of the deli at Kroger's, a woman with a cane asked me to be her friend. I was deciding between rare roast beef and ham. She rattled me so, I bought both, and some hot mustard, too. We had something in common, and I didn't like it. I went home and made a sandwich. The mustard was too hot.

I thought about getting a job. I looked over some bookstores in the neighborhood, but, though I like to read books, I do not like to yank them out of boxes or fiddle with a computer. My degree is in history, and I am drawn to facts.

I tried running. I bought a pair of white shorts, a sports bra, and blew a week's grocery money on shoes. I took it a little at a time and stayed on level territory, but running has done nothing for my spirit.

I was always thin and nervous. Now I get charley horses at night.

For the time being, I am tidying up things for spring. The windows are washed and the carpets cleaned. I've thrown out my empties, too. There's no point in letting the maid take the blame. She is a Seventh Day Adventist whose life lies flat in clean angles. Her house is willed to the church, and she lives with her sister. I suspect she saw things as they are—a long time ago.

XII

Walking Away

Think of him as a splitting headache," she said, her accent thick, her voice low.

"It's like getting rid of a headache," I mused, with my foot tucked under me, asleep. The sun was going down and the beach was orange and pink. Where do we go from here, I wondered.

The woman fingered a schnapps bottle and smiled. She was eighty years old, dressed in what looked like black cotton underwear with a laced edge at the top. Her breasts were flat. The bones in her shoulders met the tan flesh, and there was not much space between. "How many headaches have you had?" I asked myself.

The old woman's history was a secret, but I knew it. Her ex-husband took her in because it was 1945. Munich. Once she had photographed the *Bismarck*.

She had no work. Mistresses came and went in the same apartment. Now she lives with her son.

I watched her pour the schnapps. The smell was cloying. She walked the beach and picked up wood in the mornings. She played Bach in the afternoons. "You'll see," she said.

Vacations are short. The last seafood supper. The gritty drive back. Suitcases full of soggy paperbacks. Bills and brochures waiting at the neighbor's. My husband grilling his own steak. "Get me a knife, Mary."

I didn't give up or go away. I'm right here in the kitchen keeping dinner warm. Everything is a trade-off, you know. I think about it when I walk the high-school track with plugs and music in my ears and the rush of runners passing me.

The school principal is a methodical man, and he runs every day. He is spitting in the grass, his foot on the bleachers. Someone always wants to say a few words to him. The football coach. One of the fathers. Today he told me I look wonderful. In the South, things move slowly, but they seem to go somewhere.

Last year I walked with two women on my street. One got a job. The other had a third child. Now they stay in the kitchen. Next, I chose a high-powered art dealer. Our conversations were great, but her deals got in the way. Now, I have my Walkman and a drawer full of batteries. My favorite is Randy Newman. He talks in the right accents and makes me laugh.

At night when I am in bed with my husband, I don't need music or distractions. We drift around in the bedclothes and clutch at the pillows. It's a place I've wanted all my life. The windows are open, and planes from the airport split the sky.

XIII

Words to Live By

My therapist told me to tell the important people in my life how I feel. Of course, she was referring to things that count. If everyone told the truth every minute, the world would spin off into the sun. Sometimes, even getting up is a lie.

Anyway, I told my father if he ever again said how lucky I was to find someone to marry me, I'd spit in his face. Just a metaphor, but he got the point. In the past, I stayed away from him—a few letters, a phone call, a perfunctory visit once a year. It's hard enough to live, without asking for trouble.

He hasn't mentioned my marriage since. Now he tells me I foul the English language with phrases like "you know" and "okay." He doesn't speak the King's English himself. I should laugh it off, but I know more is coming. I've heard his corny philosophy too many times: "Always kick a man when he's down; you'll never get a better chance!"

I have been down a lot lately, but my brains still work, and I know the therapist made a mistake. Mean people are best left alone. He shoots cats, too, and I think it's a fine idea. A cat is an animal—dress it up as you will, or feed it warm milk.

Therapists don't know everything. Why should they want to acknowledge evil any more than the rest of us? Instead of writing form letters and reluctantly dialing the phone, now I want to bust glass.

When I was younger and full of confidence, I called my mother a name. Nobody denied it was the truth. It was Christmas. We had all had too much whiskey, except my mother. She doesn't drink. My father chased me through the snow to a neighbor's house where I put my fist through the French doors. That sobered everyone up, including the drunk who lived next door.

Where did I go from there? Paris? Chicago? No, I went back to work with a hunchback woman who got an engagement ring for Christmas. She changed the bandage on my hand and took me home to lunch. We ran a switchboard and kept things straight for six salesmen at an auto parts company. The boss made fun of us all. It's easy to find someone's weak point, if that's what you look for. It was a recession, and we bit our lips. The days all end at five o'clock anyway, and there are some things in life you have to accept.

Talk is cheap. My mother said, "Keep your mouth shut," and my father added, "Tell your troubles to Jesus." It didn't take long to see I had come to a dead end.

My therapist is letting me go with her blessing: "I've done all I can for you," she says. My husband is thrilled and promises to take me to Florida for Easter with the money he's saving. We can lie on the beach and think about the future. My father is going rabbit hunting. My husband doesn't understand his timing, but I do.

XIV

Time to Kill

I think a lot about dishwater and garbage. I have time to kill. I think about those dead boys, too. I went on the searches before they caught the killer on the bridge. Saturday mornings, my husband and I left together, a little after nine. They're putting up more high rises in Marietta, and his foreman has branched out. Sometimes we crossed the Chattahoochee within five minutes of each other.

The searchers met at a church and moved from there with a police escort. We carried big sticks to part the bushes. Evil loose in the woods. Prison guards came from Florida in a van. Nuns from Philadelphia. A librarian from the Bronx. The odds didn't seem to matter.

Each morning I read the paper and smoked my new cigars. I have settled on a brand: Henri Winterman's

Café Cremes. I like the name, and they are mild. Bacon burned and toast turned black while I considered the facts.

In April, the killer dumped a body in Executive Park, four miles from my house. Then a curfew. The next victim had been put in prison for stealing one gray glove. In my dreams, boys held by red plastic clothespins on a line float above the furniture, and every night I reel them into my chair. The windows come out of the wall, and nothing in the room is anchored down. The last boy had a face just like my husband's.

The searches continued, though the searchers decreased. The last week I went, we found a dead dog in a Hefty garbage bag and a milk jug shot full of holes. We found a red football helmet and a pair of dirty lace panties, but we did not find Timothy Hill's yellow pants in the mud from last night's rain. The body count rose to eighteen. The mayor came on television: "How long can we stand it?" He comes from five generations of preachers, and his words hit the mark.

XV
Murder

I gave up smoking and became a courtroom junkie. All around me cigarettes were lit and smashed. The smoke seemed more real than murder. But I was steadfast.

No line was too long, and some stretched around the corner and started up before dawn. There was a lot to see. I saw myself, for one thing. And others like me. I watched the defense attorney, and I saw through the words he used. Said he went fishin' with his boys in Mississippi before the sun came up. Said he wanted to see justice done. He smoked, too, and wiped his nose with a big white handkerchief. He was photographed from a dozen angles and sketched in color and black and white.

The accused killer was dull as dishwater, and the same shade. That sort of light black skin that looks like ash. He sat and passed notes, affecting courtliness, pouring water for the ladies. Waiting.

I might as well say it—that defense attorney pulled me right into his anger and his acting. I'll never know for sure which was which, but both things made me want to visit a bedroom fast. It's all those Mississippi words. And his lips. They don't go with the rest of his face or with his ridiculous hair, curved as it was, and combed over his bull-like head.

I came back to see Binder, every day—a sick man of fifty-two with stooped shoulders and a paunch. But with inflections I moved South to hear on someone's lips. Binder, you horse trader, put those gentleman's hands on the table and admit you've never had the patience for fishin', that you were drawn, like the rest of us, by something none of us can name. Speeding from the Delta in your big black car, and neither money nor justice has much to do with it. Hunger is closer to the truth.

Trials have boundaries. Isn't that what killers look for all along? In the end—steel and concrete. But the courtroom is bound by time and words. The sounds wrap themselves around the spectators and the speakers. There is a cadence to it. Time rests. We break for meals, and each day ends at four o'clock. In between, your thoughts are your own, and there is plenty to think about. Your own rage, for one thing. And, what you will do when the trial is over.

Each night I tucked away the facts and mysteries and rode the bus back home. We passed everything. Safe, inside the big wheels and steel frame, I fell asleep against the cushions.

My husband works late, so I have time for it all— the whole day, plus a bath, a beer, even peeling potatoes and cooking meat. After the meal, he listens to me repeat a few sentences from the testimony and we play Boggle until bedtime. The cubes jiggle in the cup, and words tumble out of our heads, fast. It's always a surprise to see who wins. We are evenly matched.

Every night his foreman interrupts our game. When the phone rings, I load the dishwasher to keep my mind off smoking. Building houses has a lot to do with measuring and materials. Some things don't fit, and wormy walnut is hard to find. They hired one man just to buy old barns in North Carolina.

Last night, as we were cleaning up, my husband said, "He wore a three-piece suit to school every day —from kindergarten on. My bricklayer's niece grew up with him. It all adds up: the fence, the dog, and the three-piece suit."

"So what?" I come back. "There's a difference between a freak and a killer."

"Are you sure?" he laughs.

My husband never asks why I'm at the trial. He's happy if his work clothes are hung up and the bed is made. We have no children. Let's not go into that. I do my best. A microwave is a wonderful thing, and the lettuce is fresh every day. Here, in the South, dinner still means something.

Each day brings more words and the lines are longer. Nobody else sees the killer as a person. I do. Up to a point, his life and mine are parallel. He pretended he had a job, a life. He pretended something big was going to happen, and finally it did. From there on, we part ways. All those dead boys and crazy sex.

Who knows what he was? Even the smart-ass psychologists haven't come up with a label for that part.

I have some questions, and they go back to the years before he put on the three-piece suit. How do you play with a guard dog? How much did his father like little boys? I can feel his child-self digesting the metal pieces of all those games for the junior builder, looking out the telescope and seeing through the mysteries. I'll bet he cleaned his plate and made straight A's!

I have the same questions about my own life. I can't remember anything before the first day of kindergarten. To be honest, I can't remember what happened after school until I was nine years old. It's as if I were born in chalk dust and hidden by it until my grandmother took me away. She had a wire fence and a guard dog, too. You can cut a child's mind so deep that neither doctors nor gimmicks nor true love can patch it.

Today we saw another person with an "as if" life. A friend of the killer. He came on strong. A big hello for the prosecutor. Five jobs. But none of them paid money, and he still lives with his mother, too. He marched in and ran out—the reporters on his heels— famous for one minute.

When I'm home, on the nights my husband is away, I do my thinking on my hands and knees on the kitchen floor. Pinesol surrounds me. I was right not to have children and, anyway, there's no going back now. Consider the mothers of the dead boys. The worst happens, and it happens again and again—a woman would be stupid not to expect it.

XVI

A Second Look

I've got a little more to tell you about going crazy. Let's not be skittish. I cleaned up a few details the first time around. I lied. Of course, there were nightmares. All night, wide awake, after the biographies fell off the bed. You don't doze off forever. In the end, you keep right on going until someone puts you in a hospital with a handful of pills and something stupid for every hour of the day. It all comes with three thousand calories and soggy creme pie on a tray. There's a long corridor to walk, and you need it. The medicine has side effects that jolt your body while they clear your mind. Your legs pull up, and there is no feeling like it. They give you another pill for that. It hurts while you pee. It hurts more after. Headaches play tag in your skull.

And, you know what? It's all better than being

crazy. They call what I had "disorganized." Hell, I've been disorganized all my life. My closet. My car. My makeup bag. This is different. You can't trust yourself. You think someone is mean. They're not. You think you can spot a lie. You can't.

The screen behind your eyes is gone, and you can't sort things out. You can stay away from people and cars and sit in a chair—if you try hard. But you want to get up and look for things that are lost and one thing reminds you of another until you are tempted to live like a nun in a bare room where you can concentrate on the sun and the dust. There's nowhere to go and you can't sit still. Think about it. And then forget it. I try to. What happened? Can it happen again?

Getting well is worse. All the excitement gone. The plans? They were fantasies. There's a label for everything. A second language. The words sound firm. They have their own direction. "The prognosis is good." I never ask the limits of the prognosis because I don't want to know. What is the difference between a rip and a tear?

I'm back where I started with the whole day and

the fingermarks on the walls. I've noticed the dish-
washers at the Majestic Grill. They're either crazy or
dumb or both. And they're poor. I'm not saying I
know how these women feel. I'm not saying I'm that
bad off. But some part of me is missing now, and the
prognosis is a joke.

XVII

Home Again

The trial ended in March on a black rainy afternoon. The winds blew around the deserted courthouse and parking lots, and the restaurant owners stood behind their counters and mourned.

The facts took a backseat for a while. I watched a storm from my attic window—content to be home. The attic had been a nursery for the blind children; and if Margaret were still alive, she would have turned it into a ghost story. All the doors creak like "Inner Sanctum," and the ceiling is so low you have to stoop.

Nothing happened. I don't know what I expected. It's harder without smoking, and sometimes I build a fire just to watch the twists and curls in the air. There is no shortage of kindling around here, and we have extra-long matches. I keep the lights on all day.

Around five o'clock I start supper, and the smells are some consolation. I have pewter plates. They won't break, and everything stays warm.

My husband keeps Lava soap in the kitchen sink, and that's where he goes first thing. "Mary, take your eyes off that book and give me a kiss." He has never liked to rush. I can hear the faucet drip. His foreman knows better than to call him before eight o'clock.

XVIII
The Nigger

I know a few things about "the nigger," and I learned them early. At my grandma's knee. She called him the boogeyman. I saw him in closets, in my dreams, and heard him bend the lightning rod on the tin roof we slept under. Of course I never believed all those lies scared men tell about black people. Lies I overheard at Polish weddings and company picnics in the park when I was ten. I knew "the nigger" was an invention. He was dumb, dirty, a sudden creature who might kill you in one of those dark places in your dreams. He's not there, but his image is crystal clear.

I wonder what the killer thinks about "the nigger" in his cell at the Fulton County Jail. He's not "the nigger," I'm sure. 'Cause somewhere in the puzzle inside his head, in the pounding of his blood, he has killed that "nigger" again and again. My boogeyman!

After riding downtown to take a look at the jail and getting right back on again, the bus stopped at the Majestic Grill. I tried their vegetable soup to warm up. The cash register inched along, and my head felt like someone was arm-wrestling inside it. I need a new bathrobe. Chenille would be nice. Two women without coats pass by. The rain beats on the window.

When I got home there were two letters waiting—one from Margaret's oldest daughter telling me to stay away from "near occasions of sin." Could she mean the trial? The Ritz? Another, a gallery opening. There's an artist in the neighborhood who etches nude figures on clay slabs. I have three in my bathroom and another in the front hall. Someday he'll be dragged to New York by the dealers, and he won't have time to stand beside his work, but for now he's at every opening with his wife, too. They have something that's in short supply these days. They also have Jack Daniels stashed in the back for friends who find chablis best poured over baked chicken and grapes. Now I have something to look forward to, I think, as I climb the stairs and consider where a new slab would fit in.

I keep thinking about the killer. I've read books about maniacs. Truman Capote's and two versions of Ted Bundy's story. Whodunits are a bore. Who cares who? It's why that matters. It's the first three years.

I am lying in bed now, and the rain and wind are making a hash of the curtains. I am watching carefully. I found my husband's terrycloth robe. It's clean and soft. The shutters crash against the bricks.

XIX

Where Is Pleasure to Be Found?

Forty years old. . . . I don't know what he has planned, but I bought a gray wool dress, just in case. They moved the Ritz down here. It's not the London Chop House, and it's not the old hotel in Boston, but I'm satisfied. You can pretend you are snowed in if you pull the shades, and they provide thick bathrobes and pictures that weren't stamped out of a mold. The thermostat works. Don't ask me how I know.

My friend who carries a beeper got transferred to California. Computers have their own time and place. "Everyone's young out here, and I feel old and adrift," she writes. "My window faces the freeway, and the big semis rush by on to the San Francisco valley. It's dry and ninety degrees."

"There goes my trip to the beach," I worry.

She called me. I said, "Did you know Nathanael West couldn't drive a car—right? Did you know movies are a smoke screen? They killed the best in Dorothy Parker and Dashiell Hammett. Come back! What the hell can that place do for you?"

"Be serious, Mary. Do you think I care what happened to Dashiell Hammett? He was a poor man's Hemingway in fancy clothes. He cared more about drink and Chinese whores than the printed word. I don't even know who Nathanael West was. Crawl out of your living room and breathe some fresh air, for Christ's sake!"

Now, you tell me what made her so mad! She knows damn well who West was, and the whole "Thin Man" series is on her bookshelf. I *am* breathing fresh air, and it's killing me.

XX

Another Routine

Cheer up, for Christ's sake."

"Be careful!" I come back. Another day begins. I go out for breakfast now. They serve it twenty-four hours at the Majestic Grill, and the place is usually packed. It's hot and cheap and the coffee will take your head off. My birthday is next week, and I think of nothing else.

I go to the movies alone every day at two o'clock. Nobody knows I'm here, and that in itself is fun. I see trash. Science fiction with machines that blow up fast. Horror movies, too. The killer catches the nude couple in the act. His bloody knife gleams in the sun, and thunder rolls. Sometimes I'm surprised. *Under the Volcano* had Michael Caine's voice and Mexico. Mood is everything. Which brings me to this afternoon and Cher, with her deformed son and wild life.

You know those plots!

Let me start by saying she hasn't seen the last of me. I want to memorize her face and watch her come back to her father in front of that bloody roast beef, one more time: "Yeah, your friend Vinnie did offer me a job, and he said he had a little bonus for me on the desk first. I took the bonus and told him to shove the job up his ass." I like her tone and the razors in her words. I also like her body. Long. Thin. More room for her eyes, and they say it all. They say, "It hurts bad." They say, "The doctors and the principal are just the beginning, and my father isn't even in the picture." They say, "You ain't gonna see the rest." There's something else they say, but it doesn't fit into words, and that's what I'm after at the movies.

I plan to sit in this theater and wait for Cher. I know she won't disappoint me. I thought she was a twit when she was younger. Her body-lifts. Her husbands. Her clothes. She seemed to live with feathers and sequins and expect to get somewhere. Well, she has. But it won't last long. She is forty, and they didn't touch the crow's feet in the corners of her eyes.

XXI

The Desert

Sometimes I don't have to go to the movies. I saw *The Red Desert* years ago, and I know the details of that woman's bedroom as if they were mine, now. White sheets. The walls were white, too, and something was missing. I think it was her husband. He ran a factory—all white and red and royal blue like a Mondrian painting—like no factory I've ever seen. Clean. The only dirty thing in the movie was the cloud of smoke that ruined the landscape outside the factory walls. The woman was about to scream, but she never did. Her sheets were a trap, and sex was horrible. She slept with a beefy man with blond hair over one eye. She worked in an art gallery where nothing was out of place. Her son had nightmares in his perfect modern room. I retched in the janitor's bucket when I walked out of that movie.

I can't see *The Red Desert* anymore—it went back to Sweden—so I take the new stuff, as it comes, and go on from there.

If you're looking for the point, forget it. I keep scraps like this for the off-hours, and I don't give up trying to make sense out of them.

XXII

One Trend after Another

H oly suffering Christ," he said. "What happened to the aspirin?"

"What makes you think you're the only one with a headache? They're in the china cabinet on top of the soup bowls."

If my husband had his way, this house would be organized like a military academy, and the aspirin would be on the first shelf of the medicine chest. "A" for aspirin, "B" for Bufferin. These distinctions must be made.

"Let's go to the movies, Mary."

"What will we see?"

"Does it matter?"

On the way there, we pass those fat poles that support the new road connecting the Jimmy Carter Library to Ponce de Leon. We pass Tent City and the protestors. They carry homemade signs and eat bran muffins. It's easy to kill time with good causes and ready-made friends. Nobody denies Jimmy Carter is a big balloon with SEE ME on it, and he has clashed with that special breed of Southern social climber from Druid Hills who thought they were exempt from everything. They don't want a highway running through their quiet afternoons. But the road is coming through, and nobody is exempt.

We pass Eat Your Vegetables. They have the best chocolate pie in the city. Only they make it out of carob, so you can think you'll live longer—caffeine-free. All this focus on natural food and natural body hair! Evil is natural, too. I don't see anybody on a soapbox waving a flag for it. My husband doesn't think so. He got lost in storm sash years ago, and he thinks it will save him. If the hardwood floors don't have a ripple, he forgets about the rest.

We pass the pawn shop on Euclid. Then the Berman Gallery with the nude women carved in clay. Soon we come to the Ellis Theatre. They have little tables where you can drink and watch the screen.

How long can it last?

We watch *Passage to India,* and I fall asleep. My husband's shoulder is there, and he holds my hand in his.

XXIII

Precautions

I lost things—the ordinary ones first: glasses, keys, the eye creme I paid too much for. Looking, again and again, in the same places jars you. But when I lost my car in the Rich's lot and kept walking around in the rain trying to think what pile of clothes was near what exit, I got scared. I stayed in bed for a day drinking Irish Breakfast Tea.

The next morning I walked to Plaza Drugs early. I bought four pairs of reading glasses and put them near the bed and phones. I also bought a six-inch key ring. I thought ahead and copied my addresses in a Rolodex. A rainy afternoon and the fat strokes of black ink on white paper. The eye creme turned up behind the bed. It was a frill, anyway.

What I can't shake is the feeling that something else is missing. My cigars, maybe. At the Majestic

Grill, the other customers have physical handicaps or no job to speak of. The whole place seems hung over. I see through the smoke and feel at home. I've gotten used to vegetables, Southern style, with grease and gravy. I try to be careful. You can't go against your nature, but you have to hold it in, or it will eat you alive.

XXIV
Grief

There's a lot to be said for older men. They have made a few mistakes, and they know what can't be changed. They take their time. They have to. And, in the end, their bodies are not the important part. They will hold you.

"Come for me, Mary," he whispers—hoarse with pleasure and fatigue. Why am I scared? You can ask these questions your whole life, and the answer never comes. You are left with your sweaty body and your dreams.

"Relax." You should be able to relax at the Ritz. With all the time in the world, but I end up talking about his dead wife and slow brother. Grief is easy to share. Unlike my husband, he never yells at me, but it doesn't help. I thought it would. He is sixty-five years old and has had two heart attacks. He might die in his sleep.

We talk about Dashiell Hammett. After all, he was alive then. He doesn't read books either, but he drank a few Manhattans at the Plaza when those black leather chairs were sacred. When men still wore hats, and a summer affair had the whole hot and empty city for a backdrop.

I set the limits—when my husband is in Detroit visiting his family. They are all crazy, and Polish weddings go on forever. He flies alone. "Don't get lost in that book, Mary." It does no good to cry.

XXV
The End

More and more, I dream of Margaret. Forget the ghost stories and the Doctor Dentons. Her kids are older now, and John has stayed with them. He didn't look for anyone else. You can't replace people. The house stayed a mess, and he was always there. One boy quit school, but the girls are at the University of Detroit with the Jesuits, and the oldest boy got a football scholarship to Notre Dame. John is still working on the rest.

I kept Margaret's letter and the flask. She seemed so sure of herself when she was talking about our mothers. I think of my mother, too, sometimes. Margaret sure had her pegged wrong. Those old lady's oxfords are a fooler. She had a few afternoons away from the house that must have made her doubt the possibility of an afterlife. And, all her opinions.

They were bullshit, too. She kept the real thing to herself, and it remained locked in her bedroom until the morning she died. I cleaned it out. Why should I keep my mouth shut now? Dildos. Men's suits. Jockey shorts. Wing-tips. Complete costumes. All in her size, and well worn.

"Men are bastards," she told me more than once. She missed the boat on that one, too. They go off every day, and it's hard for them to understand what waiting really means.

About the Author

Recipient of a Yaddo Writers' Fellowship, June Akers Seese is also the author of the novel *Is This What Other Women Feel Too?,* and a collection of short fiction, *James Mason and the Walk-in Closet,* both published by Dalkey Archive Press. She's currently working on a new novel, *Some Things Are Better Left to Saxophones.* She has taught at Spelman College and Callanwolde Fine Arts Center and currently lives in Atlanta.

SELECTED DALKEY ARCHIVE PAPERBACKS

PIERRE ALBERT-BIROT, *Grabinoulor.*
YUZ ALESHKOVSKY, *Kangaroo.*
FELIPE ALFAU, *Chromos.*
  Locos.
  Sentimental Songs.
IVAN ÂNGELO, *The Celebration.*
  The Tower of Glass.
DAVID ANTIN, *Talking.*
DJUNA BARNES, *Ladies Almanack.*
  Ryder.
JOHN BARTH, *LETTERS.*
  Sabbatical.
SVETISLAV BASARA, *Chinese Letter.*
ANDREI BITOV, *Pushkin House.*
LOUIS PAUL BOON, *Chapel Road.*
ROGER BOYLAN, *Killoyle.*
IGNÁCIO DE LOYOLA BRANDÃO, *Zero.*
CHRISTINE BROOKE-ROSE, *Amalgamemnon.*
BRIGID BROPHY, *In Transit.*
MEREDITH BROSNAN, *Mr. Dynamite.*
GERALD L. BRUNS,
  Modern Poetry and the Idea of Language.
GABRIELLE BURTON, *Heartbreak Hotel.*
MICHEL BUTOR, *Degrees.*
  Mobile.
  Portrait of the Artist as a Young Ape.
G. CABRERA INFANTE, *Three Trapped Tigers.*
JULIETA CAMPOS, *The Fear of Losing Eurydice.*
ANNE CARSON, *Eros the Bittersweet.*
CAMILO JOSÉ CELA, *The Family of Pascual Duarte.*
  The Hive.
LOUIS-FERDINAND CÉLINE, *Castle to Castle.*
  London Bridge.
  North.
  Rigadoon.
HUGO CHARTERIS, *The Tide Is Right.*
JEROME CHARYN, *The Tar Baby.*
MARC CHOLODENKO, *Mordechai Schamz.*
EMILY HOLMES COLEMAN, *The Shutter of Snow.*
ROBERT COOVER, *A Night at the Movies.*
STANLEY CRAWFORD, *Some Instructions to My Wife.*
ROBERT CREELEY, *Collected Prose.*
RENÉ CREVEL, *Putting My Foot in It.*
RALPH CUSACK, *Cadenza.*
SUSAN DAITCH, *L.C.*
  Storytown.
NIGEL DENNIS, *Cards of Identity.*
PETER DIMOCK,
  A Short Rhetoric for Leaving the Family.
ARIEL DORFMAN, *Konfidenz.*
COLEMAN DOWELL, *The Houses of Children.*
  Island People.
  Too Much Flesh and Jabez.
RIKKI DUCORNET, *The Complete Butcher's Tales.*
  The Fountains of Neptune.
  The Jade Cabinet.
  Phosphor in Dreamland.
  The Stain.
WILLIAM EASTLAKE, *The Bamboo Bed.*
  Castle Keep.
  Lyric of the Circle Heart.
JEAN ECHENOZ, *Chopin's Move.*
STANLEY ELKIN, *A Bad Man.*
  Boswell: A Modern Comedy.
  Criers and Kibitzers, Kibitzers and Criers.
  The Dick Gibson Show.
  The Franchiser.
  George Mills.

  The Living End.
  The MacGuffin.
  The Magic Kingdom.
  Mrs. Ted Bliss.
  The Rabbi of Lud.
  Van Gogh's Room at Arles.
ANNIE ERNAUX, *Cleaned Out.*
LAUREN FAIRBANKS, *Muzzle Thyself.*
  Sister Carrie.
LESLIE A. FIEDLER,
  Love and Death in the American Novel.
FORD MADOX FORD, *The March of Literature.*
CARLOS FUENTES, *Terra Nostra.*
  Where the Air Is Clear.
JANICE GALLOWAY, *Foreign Parts.*
  The Trick Is to Keep Breathing.
WILLIAM H. GASS, *The Tunnel.*
  Willie Masters' Lonesome Wife.
ETIENNE GILSON, *The Arts of the Beautiful.*
  Forms and Substances in the Arts.
C. S. GISCOMBE, *Giscome Road.*
  Here.
DOUGLAS GLOVER, *Bad News of the Heart.*
KAREN ELIZABETH GORDON, *The Red Shoes.*
GEORGI GOSPODINOV, *Natural Novel.*
PATRICK GRAINVILLE, *The Cave of Heaven.*
HENRY GREEN, *Blindness.*
  Concluding.
  Doting.
  Nothing.
JIŘÍ GRUŠA, *The Questionnaire.*
JOHN HAWKES, *Whistlejacket.*
AIDAN HIGGINS, *A Bestiary.*
  Flotsam and Jetsam.
  Langrishe, Go Down.
ALDOUS HUXLEY, *Antic Hay.*
  Crome Yellow.
  Point Counter Point.
  Those Barren Leaves.
  Time Must Have a Stop.
MIKHAIL IOSSEL AND JEFF PARKER, EDS., *Amerika:*
  Contemporary Russians View the United States.
GERT JONKE, *Geometric Regional Novel.*
JACQUES JOUET, *Mountain R.*
HUGH KENNER, *Flaubert, Joyce and Beckett:*
  The Stoic Comedians.
DANILO KIŠ, *Garden, Ashes.*
  A Tomb for Boris Davidovich.
TADEUSZ KONWICKI, *A Minor Apocalypse.*
  The Polish Complex.
ELAINE KRAF, *The Princess of 72nd Street.*
JIM KRUSOE, *Iceland.*
EWA KURYLUK, *Century 21.*
VIOLETTE LEDUC, *La Bâtarde.*
DEBORAH LEVY, *Billy and Girl.*
  Pillow Talk in Europe and Other Places.
JOSÉ LEZAMA LIMA, *Paradiso.*
OSMAN LINS, *Avalovara.*
  The Queen of the Prisons of Greece.
ALF MAC LOCHLAINN, *The Corpus in the Library.*
  Out of Focus.
RON LOEWINSOHN, *Magnetic Field(s).*
D. KEITH MANO, *Take Five.*
BEN MARCUS, *The Age of Wire and String.*
WALLACE MARKFIELD, *Teitlebaum's Window.*
  To an Early Grave.
DAVID MARKSON, *Reader's Block.*
  Springer's Progress.
  Wittgenstein's Mistress.

FOR A FULL LIST OF PUBLICATIONS, VISIT: www.dalkeyarchive.com